T597s

# Summer Witches

# Summer Witches

## THERESA TOMLINSON

MACMILLAN PUBLISHING COMPANY
*New York*

MAXWELL MACMILLAN INTERNATIONAL PUBLISHING GROUP
*New York* · *Oxford* · *Singapore* · *Sydney*

Macmillan Publishing Company
866 Third Avenue
New York, NY 10022
Collier Macmillan Canada, Inc.
1200 Eglinton Avenue East
Suite 200
Don Mills, Ontario M3C 3N1
First published by Julia MacRae Books, London, England
First American Edition
Printed in the United States of America

10 9 8 7 6 5 4 3 2 1

Tomlinson, Theresa
Summer witches / Theresa Tomlinson
p.   cm.
Summary: Two friends convert an old air-raid shelter into a den
and help an old woman, who teaches them sign language and herbal
medicine, to overcome her painful memories of World War II.
ISBN 0-02-789206-9
[1. Friendship—Fiction. 2. England—Fiction.] I. Title.
PZ7.T5977Su   1991
[Fic]—dc20   90-38162   CIP   AC

The text of this book is set in 12 point Goudy Old Style.
Designed by REM Studio, Inc.

*For three gardeners: Jenny, Judy, and my mum*

# Contents

# Note to the Reader

This book is set in a city in northern England. The way people live is slightly different from the way people do in the United States; some things are very different, but mostly we just use different words to talk about the same things.

The girls play the "French skipping game." This is a way to jump rope, using a very large rubber band. They eat sherbet fountains, a kind of candy made out of sweet, fizzy powder that gets sucked out of a tube with a licorice straw.

The school year is slightly different from that of American schools. In late May, there is a short vacation, the "Whitsuntide holidays," and then the children come back to school until the end of July. After that, they have the "big holidays," their main summer vacation, which lasts until the beginning of September. (During the summer people may go to the Lido, which is a sort of miniature amusement park.)

Some words are just different. The English say "sweets," when Americans say "candy." They say "lorry," when we say "truck," and "torch," when we say "flashlight." There are other words like these, but none of them is too hard to figure out.

Maybe the most important difference between England and America in this book is that England was bombed during the Second World War. Many people, especially in the big cities, were killed, and many homes were destroyed. People put air-raid shelters, little huts covered with dirt, in their backyards to protect themselves. Some of those shelters are still there now, and so are bad memories of the air-raids. Fifty years later, a leftover shelter and some of those bad memories lead to Sarah and Susanna becoming "summer witches."

# 1

# The Girl Next Door

When Susanna first came to live next door to us, I hated her. I thought she was a fat, red-haired drip, who trailed around after me. She'd moved in next door when Ruth, who'd been my best friend, went to live in another city. My cat, Stripes, liked Susanna. She was always rubbing round her knees, purring like mad, and my mother just took it for granted that I'd be friends with this new girl next door.

"Our Sarah'll walk up to school with you," she said.

She never asked me first.

Our teacher made her sit next to me in Ruth's place. "Now you won't miss Ruth," she said.

Susanna followed me around, all fat and sorrowful, and got on my nerves something terrible.

That was until the day when I was doing the French skipping game with Catherine and Tracey. I was jumping and the other two had the elastic round their ankles. I heard a lot of laughing and shouting behind me. Catherine

1

was staring at something over my shoulder, so I turned around to see.

Two of the M4 girls, who think they're superior to us, were pointing at Susanna's feet. They'd noticed her brown lace-up shoes. I must say I'd noticed them myself. They were the most clumpy, unfashionable things you'd ever seen.

"Clumpy clogs, clumpy clogs," they shouted.

Susanna backed up against the wall and stood there, red-faced and silent.

"Time she went on a diet, don't you think?"

"Clumpy clogs is a greedy guts."

One girl put her heel on the shiny, polished toe of Susanna's shoe, then stamped down hard.

Susanna never moved, but I saw something glitter on her other shoe, then another glint. She was crying, real quiet, staring down at the floor.

I couldn't stand it. My mother had bought me some disgusting shoes like that and I'd had to wear them for a week or two, then I'd refused and made her buy me a different pair.

I stepped over the elastic toward the older girls, pulling Tracey with me; I wasn't going on my own.

"Leave her alone," I said. "She's only new."

"Don't be so mean," said Tracey. She'd joined in on my side, thank goodness.

"Come on," I said to Susanna. "Come and do skipping with us."

She quickly knuckled the tears from her eyes and followed us. The two M4 girls shrieked with laughter.

"Skipping," they yelled. "She's going to do skipping."

But they linked their arms and turned away, doubled over with giggling, to look for more young kids to bait.

I thought I'd really lumbered us by getting Susanna to skip. I'd only said it because I didn't know how else to get away. I thought she'd be hopeless—so fat and miserable, and wearing those shoes.

"Can yer skip, Susanna?" asked Tracey.

She nodded her head.

"Come on then, you do the jumping."

I stood back, shaking my head, while Susanna jumped and the others stretched the elastic.

I thought it was going to be really embarrassing, but it wasn't and I couldn't have been more surprised. Once she'd got over the tears and got going, I saw that Susanna really could skip.

Tracey and Catherine stared at each other, then at me.

"Hey, that's ace," said Catherine.

Susanna did some new jump that I'd never seen before and suddenly she looked different. She threw her head back and her red hair streamed out behind like a flag. Her face glowed, and those clumpy shoes simply flew up and down, so fast you could hardly see them.

"Hey," I shouted. "Slow down, show me how you do that one."


That day we walked home from school together and I told her about the lace-up shoes I'd had. I told her how I'd nagged and nagged at my mum until she gave in and bought me a pair of smart slip-ons.

"The trouble is, my mum really believes in good shoes," said Susanna. "She doesn't mind about me clothes. She's always going to garage sales for clothes, but she gets really cross about having good shoes."

I nodded and I did understand. My mum is always getting us clothes from garage sales, too, and there's some really awful things.

As we got to our house, my cat, Stripes, jumped onto my shoulder from our front wall. She waits there for me every teatime. Sometimes I think she's the only one who really likes me—all the time. Susanna laughed as Stripes pushed her nose into my face, giving me wet, furry kisses. I laughed, too, and wondered why I'd ever thought Susanna a drip.

"Do you want to play round at our house?" I asked.

She nodded, dead keen, and I knew I'd been a bit mean to her. We walked around the back of our house and found my mother there with a terrible mess of rubbish spread over the garden.

"What's going on?" I asked.

My mother wiped a dirty hand through her hair.

"I'm wondering if it's such a good idea after all," she said. "Your dad said he was going to pull out the old shelter to give us more garden space, but it's full of old rubbish that's been there for years and that has to be cleared first."

"What a mess," I said, and started picking about in it. Susanna and Stripes followed me.

"That cat," said my mum. "Back again. Where she

goes during the day, I don't know; she's never here, but come four o'clock she's back on the dot."

"Aaah, she's lovely," said Susanna.

"Hey, there's that scooter. I wondered where that was." I pulled out a rusting scooter with a wheel missing. I'd had it when I was younger.

"Now don't start that," begged my mum. "It's all rubbish and it's all going. I've had enough trouble keeping Jonathan out of it without you starting."

Jonathan, my three-year-old nuisancy brother, came out of the back door just at that moment.

"Me want that," he shouted.

"Now look what you've done," said my mum.

"What's he got in his hand? You're always buying him sweets when I'm not here."

"From my friend." Our Jon waved something brown and sticky at me.

"Yes, it's not me," said my mum. "It's Miss Lily down the road, the lady he calls his friend. She's given him homemade fudge."

Susanna tickled our Jon's stomach. He giggled and clutched his belly, then stuck it out again for more.

"Well, it's not fair," I insisted. "Can I have some money to go down to the shops?"

"I suppose so."

My mum suddenly looked tired and pale. She'd a dirty smudge on her cheek.

"Just don't start pulling things out of this mess."

"I won't," I promised, and climbed carefully out. Mum fished in her pocket for some change.

"Here, get something for Susanna, too."

We walked down our street to the shop on the corner and I started telling Susanna who lived in each house.

There was the more modern house next door to ours. My dad said there'd once been two old houses there. They got bombed during the war and someone got killed.

I didn't know all the people down our road, but I knew most. I'd lived here as long as I could remember.

"That's Jennifer Wainwright's. It's so clean and smart her mum won't let anyone in to play. This is where the Forbes's bulldog gets you, if you're not careful."

We got to the house with the overgrown brambles covering half the front, and a brambly tunnel down the side.

"Duck down," I said. "Duck down."

Susanna looked a bit surprised, but she copied me. "Why?"

"It's the witch's house," I told her. "Well, she's Miss Lily really but I call her a witch. She's a bit funny; she waves her arms about and pulls faces. She scares me. Sometimes there's delicious smells coming from her kitchen."

"Well?" said Susanna.

"She's trying to lure children in so she can push them into her oven and cook them."

I crept past, keeping down. Susanna followed me, then we both got up giggling and ran down to the shops.

We bought ourselves sherbet fountains. I love sherbet fountains; they're my favorite sweet, although my mum complains about them dropping sticky white powder everywhere. It's so exciting the way you suck and think nothing's coming, then suddenly a great lump of sherbet shoots into your mouth and chokes your throat with the sweet tingling taste that makes your eyes water.

I looked at Susanna, sucking her cheeks in and coughing and giggling, and I thought what a smashing new friend I'd got.

# ꒰ 2 ꒱

# The Old
# Air-Raid Shelter

When we got back to our house, my dad was there, already clearing out the shelter. He was carrying the rubbish from the back, down the side passage, to dump it in the front.

"Hey you two, what about giving us a hand?"

I pulled a face but Susanna had already started picking bits up, so I thought we might as well help. We hadn't anything else to do.

It wasn't too bad really and I did keep discovering interesting old things that I'd forgotten about. It was quite hard to throw them away, but Mum was being ruthless.

At last it had all gone. Susanna went peeping into the old air-raid shelter that had been stuffed full of rubbish for so long. It was a wartime shelter, sunk a little way into the ground and covered with earth and rocks and weeds. My dad called it the Anderson shelter. It had that wavy corrugated iron bolted across the entrance, and the walls inside were corrugated iron, too. You had to climb down a small wooden stepladder to get in.

I followed Susanna, realizing that I'd never had a really good look in it. We'd gradually made it our rubbish dump; anything we didn't want got slung inside. I couldn't remember it ever being empty before.

It was dark and dirty down there.

"It's got a window," Susanna said. "You can't see that from outside."

I looked where she was pointing, and thought that she was right. Two filthy closed curtains hung on a wire coil, bolted into the metal. I pulled one greasy curtain with my fingertips, and we both laughed. There was no window, just a kid's picture, painted on the iron, all grubby with dust.

"Some window," I said.

Susanna pressed her face up close to the painted bit, holding back the other curtain.

"There's flowers and trees. Some little kid has painted a garden."

As I turned, I bumped into a wooden plank that Dad hadn't pulled out. I tugged at the wood but it wouldn't move.

"It's part of the shelter," said Susanna, and she pulled at it, too. "There's another one here." She trailed her hand along the planks.

"Ugh. They're covered in dust. They're like two shelves built into the wall."

"I wish we could see better," I said. "It's weird but it's interesting, isn't it?"

"Is there a light?" Susanna asked.

"I don't think so . . . but I've got a torch. I could bring it in."

I fetched the torch and a bit of string.

"I thought we could hang it up, then it'd be like a light."

"Yes, there's a nail up here on the top of these shelves."

We managed to hang the torch from the nail near the low roof, then we turned around and stared. The light had transformed the shelter. The creepy darkness had gone, leaving it cozy and warm, a place of safety.

A heavy black curtain hung from a rail that stretched right across the entrance. I pulled it and it came unwillingly, sticking in places and showering us with rust.

"That looks better," I said.

"There's another painting here, on the end wall." Susanna was rubbing at the dirt with her fingers. "It's a good one, this is. There's a roaring fire in a fireplace, with a clock and ornaments on the mantelpiece. It'd be great if it wasn't so mucky."

"There's another here," I said, tilting the torch to shine on it. "It's a picture of a table, with cakes and jellies, and sweets and things. This one would be good, too, if it was cleaned."

Susanna gave a sigh. "It's a funny place to find all these things, but someone has made it feel like a little home."

I knew just what she meant. "I could stay here for ages, if it wasn't so dirty."

Suddenly something clicked in my head and I got an idea that I knew was going to be a lot of trouble, but once it was there I couldn't get rid of it.

"Let's clean it up," I said. "Let's clean it up and make it our den." I knew my dad was going to pull it out and fill the place with soil; he wanted to have a small vegetable plot. He'd been planning it for ages and he'd just got round to doing something about it . . . but I couldn't help getting my idea. Since my friend Ruth had moved away, I'd been miserable and bored but now suddenly I had plans and energy. I was bursting with energy.

Susanna understood. "Oh, it'd be great," she said. "It'd be a lot of work, mind. We'd really have to work hard, and wasn't your dad going to do something with it?"

I nodded and thought hard. The next day would be Saturday, but my dad works in his bookshop on Saturdays so he couldn't start pulling it out then.

"We mustn't tell them," I said. "If we ask, they'll say no and stop us. We'll have to do it secretly."

"Mmm. That'll be difficult."

"My mum will go out shopping in the morning," I said, "and take Jonathan with her. If we said we were going to play at your house, we could get some cleaning things and get on with it while she's out."

"They'll find out later."

"Yes, they will, but if we could get it looking really nice first, they'd see how much work we'd done. Well, perhaps we'd have a chance."

Susanna nodded. "It's exciting," she said. "And it's even better doing it in secret."

# Ꭷ 3 Ꭶ

# Our Den

The next morning I was up early and restless. I wanted to get on with our job, but my mum and dad seemed determined to stay in bed longer than usual. Then, when my dad had at last got up and gone to open up, my mum seemed to take ages getting herself organized and ready to go out.

"Come with me, Sarah, and help me carry the stuff," she said.

"Oh, Mum, I promised I'd go round to Susanna's house."

"Well, why don't you go then? Instead of hanging around, getting in my way."

"I'm going."

\*     \*     \*

When I got round to Susanna's, we went upstairs to her bedroom so we could peep out of the window and see when my mum had gone.

At last I heard the thud of our front door and saw our Jon running out of the gate.

We went downstairs to Susanna's mum. "We're playing in Sarah's garden," Susanna called as we went past.

I found our back-door key hidden under its brick, and we collected buckets, mop, cloths, and cleaning liquid from our kitchen.

The darkness hit us as we went into the shelter and it took us a while to find the torch still hanging from its string. When at last we switched it on and stared around, I nearly changed my mind. There was so much dust and filth and so many spiders, I couldn't see how we could possibly sort it out. Susanna wouldn't have any of that. She shook my arm.

"Come on then, we haven't long. Let's take these curtains down and wash them."

I knew she was right, and started to work with furious energy. We had to slide the curtains off the stretchy wire coil and that took a bit of doing. The curtains stayed a dreary gray when we put them into the water.

"Leave them to soak while we do the rest," said Susanna.

All right, Miss Bossy Boots, I thought. I didn't say it, just got on. We hadn't time to waste arguing. We set to work sweeping, mopping, and wiping, and trying not to fuss as spiders ran over our shoes. Our Stripes discovered us and decided to join in. She kept sniffing and poking into the corners and being a nuisance in a nice sort of way.

Susanna stopped in the middle of wiping the wooden planks and stared at them.

"They're beds, bunk beds."

I stopped my work and looked. They were just wide enough to slide a mattress on. "So they are," I said. "We can lie on them when we've done. We'll need a rest."

Cleaning the paintings was the best but also the most difficult bit. We had to wash them really gently, with squeezed-out cloths. We still couldn't stop some of the old paint from crumbling off. It was wonderful to see how good the paintings looked when we'd got them done. The flames in the fireplace blazed golden and red, and the garden picture was beautiful. You could see climbing roses, carefully painted onto a wiggling green stem, and tiny daisies in the grass, each with separate petals and proper daisy leaves.

I looked at my watch and realized that time was passing.

"Mum'll be back soon. I want to bring things from my bedroom. We've got to make it look great, if they're going to let us keep it."

So I raided my bedroom and brought down two cushions, my fluffy rug, and an old blanket. Susanna brought her little kid's basket chair, and her old dolls' tea set.

We draped the blanket over the bottom bunk.

"We need a table and tablecloth," Susanna said.

I fetched a flowery tea towel from our kitchen, which looked really nice and fresh, and draped it over a cardboard box, then put out the dolls' tea set.

"I saw the old witch out there," I told Susanna. "She's standing by our gate, staring down the side of our house."

"Oh, is that her?" said Susanna. "I did see a woman by your gate when I went back to my house. She looked a bit nosy about what we were doing. Perhaps she's putting the evil eye on us."

"Oh, shut up," I said. "She gives me the creeps."

At last we decided to stop. I brought some lemonade from our house, which we poured into the little cups on our table and sat down grinning at each other. The place smelled clean and looked good.

"I'm whacked," I said.

"Here, we deserve this," said Susanna, passing me the bottle. She got up and went to look at the soaking curtains.

"They're checked," she said.

"No, let's see."

Appearing through the grime and filth was a green-and-white-checked pattern.

"Look at this," said Susanna, pointing to rows of tiny cross-stitch embroidery.

"That must have taken ages to do." I stroked it with one finger.

Suddenly the door was pushed open and our Jon poked his head in. As he looked from me to Susanna and then at the shelter, a big smile lit his face. Although he was little he knew what we were doing.

"Sarah here," he yelled.

We stood there silent as my mum appeared, feet first.

She stuck her head in and looked around, taking in all the details, the tables, the cups, the blanket, the buckets, and the mop.

"I don't know what your dad will say," she said.

Dad stood in the middle of the shelter, examining our work. "Oh no," he groaned. "Oh no."

Just then the torch flickered and went out completely; the battery had died. We had to struggle out in the dark.

"Please, Dad," I said, desperately trying to think of the right thing to say.

"Oh no," he kept groaning. "Oh no."

The next morning I came down early before my parents. I felt miserable and a bit guilty. I'd known my dad's plans for his vegetable garden. I thought we must have been mad to do all that work when I knew he was going to pull the shelter out. I stood on our porch, which is a newer bit that's been built onto the back of the house. I stared sadly across to our shelter. Then I noticed a small white cable running out of the shelter, by the steps, and around the garden wall, right up to the porch where I was standing. It was all neatly clipped to the wall and it actually went under the door into our kitchen. I turned around and followed it into the house. I traced it back to an electric socket in the baseboard. I couldn't believe it. I ran out to the shelter, down the steps, and went inside. I followed the cable with my fingers, then clicked on an electric light bulb which was hanging from a hook neatly fixed into the top of the bunks.

I ran back into the house and up the stairs two at a time.

"Dad, Dad," I shouted. "I've found the light. Can we have the shelter? Can we have our den?"

"Ooh, don't shout. Not at this time of the morning."

"Oh, Dad. Does it mean we can have our den?"

"Yes, you can have it. I'll dig my garden when you've left home."

I hugged him tight. "You're the best dad," I said. "The best."

# ❦ 4 ❧

# The Secret

Susanna and I really moved into the shelter properly. We made our bunks as comfortable as we could and brought all sorts of things from our houses: rugs, cushions, pens, and even our old teddies. We spent most of our evenings there. When my mother had washed and ironed the curtains for us, they turned out to be crisp green-and-white checks with red-and-blue criss-cross embroidery around the bottom. We really wanted to sleep in the shelter, but Mum said we'd have to wait until the summer holidays.

I showed my dad the funny paintings, and asked him who could have done them.

"I'll ask Rose," he said. "She'll know of course."

I wondered for a moment why Rose was bound to know, then I realized that Dad always asked Rose about everything. He said she was keen on local history.

Rose is the big lady who works in our library. Sometimes she goes into my dad's shop and they talk for hours and hours, mainly about their favorite subject: books, especially old books. As far as they're concerned, the older the book the better. Dad will get out some old book that he's bought and show it to Rose. They both get very excited and turn the pages slowly and carefully as though it's the most wonderful thing you could ever find.

One night, when Susanna had gone home, I was lying on the top bunk in our den with Stripes beside me. She was digging and poking at something between the boards.

"What are you doing, mad cat?" I said. Then I noticed a tiny corner of brown paper just sticking up from a joint in the wood.

I poked at it but couldn't get it out.

"What have you found, puss?" I said.

I fished in my pockets and pulled out a bobby pin. With a lot of scraping and poking, at last it came free. It was folded paper, all brown and dirty, folded tight and small with brown gummed paper sticking the edges together.

I sat up now, really interested, and broke the paper seal.

I had to open the paper out again and again. It was quite a big piece, but all falling apart, with being so old. I spread it flat and tried to read the faded writing, big loopy writing like a little kid's. It said:

> *This is a secret document*
> *I am the lady of the secret place*

*Nobody will tell*
*My secret document will never be found.*

The paper started to shake; a shiver ran from my hands up into my shoulders. *My secret document will never be found.* The words stuck in my head. I read them over and over again. It's just a child's game, I told myself. There must have been a child sheltering here during the war. The child must have been bored and written this silly note to pass the time; but still my hands shook. I carefully folded up the note and pushed it back into its hiding place. I picked up our Stripes and, hugging her warm and purring to my chest, I went back into the house.

The next day Susanna came round to play in the shelter as usual. All the time we were there I was bursting to tell her what I'd found. I kept starting to say it, but I'd get as far as her name and then those words came back to me.

*Nobody will tell*
*My secret document will never be found.*

"Is there something up with you?" Susanna asked.
"No, course not," I lied.
"I'm good at keeping secrets," said Susanna. She kept looking at me and waiting for me to say something.
I wanted to tell her so much, but I couldn't.
Then our Stripes started jumping onto the top bunk,

scratching around up there. I couldn't stand being in the shelter any longer. I pulled Stripes down.

"I'm fed up with playing in here," I said. "Let's go in my bedroom for a change."

Susanna looked surprised and a bit hurt. "I thought you loved it here."

"Well, I did . . . but I'm fed up with it now."

I pulled back the curtain and went out. Susanna followed me slowly. As I climbed up the steps, I saw the witch woman standing by our gate again, staring down the side of our house. I thought she was staring at us, then I saw she was looking straight past us. It seemed to be our shelter that she was interested in.

I nudged Susanna. "I hate her. What's she doing standing there looking at us, the old witch."

Susanna giggled. "She's not really a witch," she said. "My mum told me that she's deaf and she can't speak."

"Yes, I know really. I suppose I should be sorry for her. Our Jon loves her, but I hate the way she's staring. Sometimes she seems to be smiling at me, in a horrid way, and she sort of grunts. She gives me the shivers."

I thought I'd feel better when we got up into my bedroom, away from that worrying note, but I didn't.

Susanna peeped from behind my curtains.

"She's still there."

"Look at her," I said. "She makes me feel like Rapunzel. You know, Rapunzel was locked in a tower by an ugly old witch. I feel like Rapunzel looking down from her tower and the witch won't let me out. Silly old witch."

"She's not really old," said Susanna. "Older than

my mum or yours, but not really old. She's got nice black hair."

"It's got gray bits in," I insisted, "and she always has it pulled back in a bun, all tight and smooth—that's how witches have their hair in the daytime. It's to disguise them, you see."

Susanna laughed. I knew I was being stupid, and even nasty, but finding that note had made me feel worried and somehow guilty. I couldn't seem to help behaving badly.

"Open the window and shout at her," I said.

"Oh no," said Susanna, laughing more than ever. "You do it. I daren't."

I looked around first. I knew I'd get into terrible trouble with my mother if she caught me. I opened the window just a little way and shouted, "Go away, witch!" then slammed the window shut and we both slipped down onto the floor, giggling like mad.

At last when we'd stopped and our stomachs ached, Susanna pulled herself up to peep out of the window again. She clapped her hand to her mouth. "She's still there."

"Of course she is," I said. "I wouldn't have done it if she could have heard me. She can't tell."

But just then the witch looked straight up at us, straight at me, I thought. Still nodding her head, she raised her arm and waved and smiled; a terrible smile, lonely and lost. Then she hurried away to her own house.

I pretended I hadn't seen. We stood there, silent for a moment. The fun had gone and I was ashamed.

# ❧ 5 ❧

# The Witch's House

The Whitsuntide holidays began and we had two weeks off from school. The weather was warmer and we begged our mothers to let us sleep in the shelter, but they wouldn't. "In the big summer holidays," they said.

One afternoon, Susanna was at home and I was bored. My mother asked me to take our Jonathan down to the shops for some sweets.

"You get yourself some, too," she said.

"I thought he always had treats from his friend," I said.

"Oh, Miss Lily. Yes, she does spoil Jon. She usually stops by the front gate and makes a great fuss of him, but we haven't seen her today. He looks out for her now. I've often asked her to come in, but she won't."

Little brothers are such a nuisance. If Susanna had

one of her own she wouldn't think our Jon so cute. Still, I thought I'd better take him out; at least I'd get some sweets myself.

On the way back, Jon ran ahead of me, but he stopped just in front of the witch's house, staring at the window.

"I'm going to see my friend," he shouted, and before I could stop him he'd run down the side through the bramble tunnel and disappeared into the house.

Typical, I thought. Little brothers. They always run off where you don't want to go when you're supposed to be in charge of them.

I stood by the witch's gate, looking up the path. Stupid boy, I thought. Serves you right if you get stuffed full of gingerbread and shoved into an oven.

Just then I heard our Jonathan's voice shouting my name. I hated going down that path, but I thought I'd better. I remembered how I'd shouted out of our window. Had she noticed that or not? The door down the side passage opened and Jonathan leaped out.

"Sarah, Sarah, something wrong with my friend."

I couldn't understand what the matter was . . . but something was terribly wrong. Everything was wrong. The witch was sitting at the kitchen table, but the table was covered with broken china and mess. Dust covered her hair. A chair was overturned and I could hear the trickle and drip of water. The witch sat still just staring. Her lips didn't move, but a horrible groaning came from her throat. I saw that she was shaking, her whole body trembling. I was so shocked I couldn't move or think what to do. Then Jonathan put his arms around the witch's waist, hugging her tight.

"My friend's poorly," he said.

Suddenly the witch looked down at him, as though she'd just woken up, and the groaning stopped. She stared at him, then smiled. She looked over at me and started to fish in her pocket; she brought out a small notepad and a pencil stub. She put the pad down on the table and started to write in among all the mess. Her hand shook like mad and she kept stopping, then trying again. It seemed like ages, but at last she finished and held a note out to me.

"Bomb in my kitchen," it said.

I looked around and, although it seemed a bit silly, it looked like a bomb to me, too. I took the note.

"I'll get my mum," I said. I couldn't think what else to do.

I held my hand out to Jonathan, but he shook his head. "I'm looking after my friend," he said. The witch, who I knew wasn't really a witch, put her hand on his head and stroked his hair.

I turned from the door and ran without stopping till I got to our house. I burst into the kitchen.

"Jonathan's at the witch's house and something awful has happened."

My mum stared at me. "The witch's house?"

"Oh, you know. Miss Lily."

My mum looked really angry. "Don't ever let me hear you say that again."

I couldn't seem to get it through to Mum that she was needed.

"You've got to come, though."

"Good heavens no. If Jonathan's with Miss Lily, he'll be fine."

The words wouldn't come out fast enough. I held out the note. "No, you must come. Something terrible . . . Miss Lily . . . covered in dust."

At last she took notice. She suddenly grabbed the note and was heading for the door before I could say anything else.

"Stay here and mind the house," she shouted and was gone.

I flopped down onto a chair. I was glad to be left there and not have to face that horrible mess again. I sat still for a while, just calming down. I noticed the bit of paper, Miss Lily's note, where my mother had dropped it near the door. Something about it bothered me. I went over and picked it up. I glanced down at the writing and read it again. "Bomb in my kitchen." I looked at the writing, all shaky but with big loops; sort of familiar in some way. Then suddenly I realized what it was. I did know that writing; I had seen it before. I wasn't calm anymore and couldn't keep that other note secret. I'd burst if I didn't tell someone right away. I rushed straight around to Susanna's house and hammered on her door.

"What's up?" asked Susanna. "You've got a dirty face."

I grabbed her hand. "Come in the shelter," I said. "I've just got to tell you. I can't keep it to myself anymore."

Susanna opened her eyes wide, then narrowed them. "I knew there was something." she said.

*   *   *

"Hold this," I said to Susanna, giving her the note from Miss Lily's pad.

I climbed straight up onto the top bunk and found the old note. It had a corner sticking out between the boards. I think Stripes had been poking at it again. I pulled it out and opened it, tearing a bit, I was in such a hurry.

"Look at that," I said. "Now tell me if it's the same."

"The same?"

"Same writing, not the same words of course."

She looked at one note, then back at the other. She caught her breath. "Oh . . . A secret document, it says . . ."

"But look at the writing," I insisted.

She looked at me a bit puzzled, but she nodded. "Yes, it's the same. But whose . . . ?"

I tried to slow down so that I could explain it all to her. It was difficult because I felt so excited and there was a lot to tell, but she listened and asked questions and at last she understood.

"It is a creepy note," she said. "I'd have felt scared if I'd found it, and it must have been the witch who wrote it. You don't think she creeps in here when we're out, do you?"

"No," I said. "The loops are the same and the way the letters are done, but I think the old note looks more like a child's writing. In the other one it's sort of shaky, too."

Susanna agreed. "Perhaps she came here when it was the war. She might have come here to shelter, when they were dropping bombs. Do you remember how she was looking at the shelter the other day?"

I nodded. "I feel awful about shouting at her that time, even if she didn't hear. I feel bad about calling her a witch, too. If you'd seen her today, Susanna . . . She looked little and sad and scared."

Susanna thought for a moment. "Well, we won't call her a witch anymore. I didn't really like doing it. She's Miss Lily, isn't she, and we'll try to be nice to her from now on."

# 6

# A Long Time Ago

Susanna and I sat there in the shelter for what seemed a long time. We kept looking at the notes, worrying about them, and wondering what was happening down at Miss Lily's house. Then at last we heard the sound of Jonathan's tricycle.

"What's happened?" I said as I climbed up the shelter steps.

"My friend's better," he said, and rode off around the front.

"That's not much use."

"Ask your mum." Susanna pushed me from behind.

We went into the kitchen and found my mother making herself a cup of tea.

"Well?" I asked. "Well?"

"It's all right. It wasn't a bomb. Of course it wasn't a bomb, but you do hear things and it did shake me up a bit when you showed me that note."

"But what was it then? Tell us what it was."

"Come on, girls, sit down and have a cup of tea. I feel as though I need one."

"For goodness' sake, tell us what it was, Mum."

"It was a burst water pipe, up in Miss Lily's bathroom, above her kitchen."

Susanna and I looked at each other and groaned. A burst water pipe didn't seem very dramatic. We sat down and accepted the cups my mum pushed over to us.

"Poor Miss Lily is very shaken, very shaken indeed, but she's all right now. We rang Rose at the library and she's putting her to bed, and the plumbers have arrived to sort out the pipes."

"We've had a burst pipe," said Susanna. "It was at our old house."

"But it was a horrible, horrible mess," I said.

"Yes it was . . . terrible," Mum agreed. "It happens like that sometimes. The pipe had burst and water had leaked into the bathroom floorboards. Water must have been dripping down from the ceiling, but of course Lily didn't hear it. The water brought the kitchen ceiling down. That's what made the mess and terrified poor Lily. I don't think she realized what had happened."

"Why's Rose there? Do people always send for Rose when something goes wrong?"

"Yes, they do seem to, don't they . . . but Rose is Miss Lily's sister. Rose and Lily live together. Where did you think Rose lived? You didn't think she had a bed at the back of the library, did you?"

Susanna and I both giggled. I did think that when I was little.

"Mind you, I wouldn't put that past Rose," said Mum. "What she has in that library is nobody's business. First it was the pets' corner, then the fancy dress, now the latest thing is cups of coffee, I hear."

"Dad said he was going to ask Rose about our shelter," I remembered.

"Yes," said Mum. "Rose is likely to know who lived here during the war, if anybody does."

There was a light tap on the front door. When Mum went to answer, we heard that it was Rose herself.

"Come in, Rose," Mum was saying. "How is she?"

"Fast asleep," said Rose. "I gave her chamomile tea; she finds that soothing. I just wanted to say thank you for your help. You've been so kind."

Mum pushed a chair out for Rose to sit down.

"It was the children who found her. Sarah came rushing up here to get me."

"That was good of you, Sarah."

"Oh, it was our Jon really," I said.

"Still, I'm glad you fetched your mother. Lily was so shocked she could have been sitting there all afternoon."

"I tried to get her to come here," said Mum. "She wouldn't, though."

"No," said Rose, her face going all worried. "No, she wouldn't do that. You see, Lily and I have sad memories of this house. We used to live here when we were little, during the war."

I caught my breath and nudged Susanna.

"Well, goodness," said Mum. "We had no idea."

"No," said Rose. "Of course you wouldn't. I've never mentioned it. You see, something happened long ago, during the war, something Lily has never quite got over and I've never liked to talk about. But I want to tell you now, then you'll understand why Lily was so shocked this morning and why she thought it was a bomb."

"Oh, I think I'm beginning to see now," said Mum. "We'd heard that a bomb fell on the house next door during the war, but we didn't know then that you and Lily had lived here. Of course if you were here . . ."

"Yes," said Rose. "That's it. You see, Lily and I often used to sleep in the shelter. We enjoyed it at first. We loved being in there. Our parents only came in after the siren had gone, but we slept there sometimes just for fun. It was our special place, our secret den. But then the bomb fell. It hit the house next door, but our mother was just coming out to us. She'd been fetching a drink for Lily. The blast caught the back of our house and the porch fell down on her."

We all stared in horrified silence.

"I heard that someone had been killed, but I never thought . . ." said Mum.

"The people from next door, the Pearsons, they were all right. They were in the shelter—they came in with us on bad nights. Well, it's all a long time ago now, but it affected Lily very badly; she was so close to our mother. I'm afraid that's why she won't come into your house. My father took us to Derbyshire to live with his mother afterward."

"Poor Lily," said my mother. "There's no wonder she was so upset today. It must have seemed like a bomb and it would have brought it all back to her."

Rose nodded. "It happened to a lot of people of course. I think it's just as well you know. Lily accepts my mother's death now. The trouble is that she still thinks she was to blame, still after all these years. She can't forget that she sent Mother out to fetch a drink of water for her."

"She's not to blame. How terrible for her to think that. I'll pop round tomorrow and bring our Jon. He cheers her up," Mum promised.

"That would be good of you. Now, I must get back and see that she's all right," said Rose, getting up to go.

I plucked up my courage. After all Rose had just said, I wasn't sure I should ask now but there was something I still wanted to know. "Was it you and Lily that did the paintings in the shelter?"

Rose suddenly smiled. "Oh, are they really still there? I thought someone would have got rid of them years ago."

"We've cleaned them, ever so carefully," I said.

"We really like them," said Susanna.

"Yes, they've been having a lovely time in that old shelter," said Mum.

"That's wonderful," said Rose. "Lily and I had some happy times there, too." She went out, leaving us thoughtful and sad.

"I'm going back to the shelter," I said. Susanna got up and followed me.

We just sat there quietly for a while, looking around at the paintings and the wooden bunks. Looking at it differently. Seeing two young girls making a wonderful, safe hideaway. Finding a bit of fun and comfort during the frightening wartime years.

"I don't know what I'd do if my mum died," said Susanna. "I can't bear to think of it."

"No," I said. "Me neither. It's all made me feel so sad."

"It's strange that they made a den here, just like us." Susanna stood up and ran her hand along the rough bunk planks. "Strange that two young girls slept here and . . . and liked it just like we do."

"Yes, and those two girls are now Miss Lily and Rose. It should feel creepy and nasty in here now we know what's happened, but it doesn't; it still feels good and safe."

"Yes," said Susanna. "Perhaps if we could get Miss Lily to come in here, she might feel better about it all."

"You must be mad," I said.

# ༄ 7 ༄

# The Sort of Person Who'd Understand

The next morning my mum took our Jon round to see Miss Lily. I felt as though I wanted to go, too, but I was still uncomfortable about finding that note, even though we knew that it had been written by a child, and even though we knew she was not a witch but a poor sad lady who'd had terrible things happen to her. Still I wished I hadn't found the note. It was too secret, too private. I couldn't get it out of my mind.

Susanna came round and we tidied up our shelter, then sat looking at the notes.

"I think you should show the note to Rose," said Susanna. "I don't know her very well, but she seems the sort of person who'd understand."

How come Susanna always knows exactly what to do? I thought. "Yes, I could tell Rose. Mind you, Rose isn't the sort of person you mess with. She never has any fooling in the library. Do you know, I once saw that Gary Fox and his gang swinging on the library door."

"Oh no, not him," Susanna said, rolling her eyes.

"Yes," I said. "He was trying to trip people up as they went in and out. I showed him my fist when I went in and he didn't try tripping me."

Susanna giggled.

"But when I'd got my books and I'd taken them up to the desk, there he was sitting at a table, good as gold, looking like a little angel helping Rose to mend torn books."

"No," said Susanna, holding her sides laughing.

"Oh yes, and I've seen him there since, sorting books back onto their shelves, all helpful and quiet. No one would think he's the worst boy in our class."

"Did your mum say Rose was making cups of coffee in the library?"

"Yes. That's her latest thing. She's always got people in there, talking for hours, and she often ends up making them coffee anyway. I think she's decided to make it official."

"Well, shall we go to see Rose?" said Susanna. "She must know Miss Lily better than anyone, and we're not messing around. We're serious, aren't we?"

"You're right." I folded the old note carefully and put it into my pocket as we set off for the library.

We wandered past the shops and knocked on my dad's window at him. It was only as we walked up the path to the library and saw it all dark and gloomy that I remembered.

"Oh no, it's Thursday. It's closed on Thursday. I'm always forgetting that."

We walked back home feeling dismal. Now we'd got this idea of talking to Rose, I wanted to get it done. My mum and Jon were there when we got back.

"I thought you'd gone to Miss Lily's," she said.

"Yes, we've been there. She's absolutely fine again and she's gone out to her class."

"Oh. Is Rose there?"

"Yes, of course, it's Thursday."

"Is she by herself?"

"Not exactly," Mum smiled. "I think she wishes she was. She's got the plasterer there, fixing the ceiling, but he won't stop telling Rose about this girlfriend of his who's left him."

Susanna nodded at me and we both set off down the street, turning in at the bramble tunnel that led to Rose and Lily's door.

I suddenly felt a bit nervous, standing on the doorstep. I remembered the story about the little mermaid going to consult the sea witch. I thought I knew how she must have felt, but Susanna gave me a nudge and I rang their doorbell.

As soon as Rose opened the door we could hear banging from inside.

"Oh good," said Rose. "Just the people I wanted to see."

That surprised us a bit.

"We . . . er, wondered if we could talk to you?" I said. "It's about Miss Lily." I don't think Rose could hear.

I tried to shout over the banging, but I felt as though what I wanted to say should be private. It all seemed very awkward.

"Just a minute," said Rose, and disappeared into the house. She came back a moment later and shut the door behind her. At last we could hear properly.

"You know, after we'd talked about the old shelter and our paintings, and how you've made a den in there, I began to think that I'd love to come and have a look at it all."

"Oh yes," we said, pleased at the idea.

# ❧ 8 ❧

# The Circle Will Be Completed

Rose had to duck her head to get inside.

"My goodness, I can't slip in here like I used to," she said.

She stepped in and we put the light on and drew the curtain behind her. She just stood there in the middle of the den, quite still, looking around at everything. Then she moved to the bottom bunk and sat down. She stared at the table and chair, her face all tense and serious. I'd never seen Rose look like that before. Suddenly she smiled.

"It's lovely. It's lovely, but strange. You've made it very much the same as it was when we were here. We had the table there, and our chair. We even had our old dolls' tea set on it and these . . . these really are the same curtains. The curtains my mother made, and all this cross-stitch embroidery was done by Lily. She was good at that, even when she was very young."

Susanna sat down on the bottom bunk beside Rose. "They were all black when we found them, but Sarah's mum washed them properly for us."

They sat there side by side. Rose had dark hair, with a thick fringe cut straight across her forehead, lightly striped with gray, like Miss Lily's; but Rose was not like her sister in any other way. Lily was thin and delicate, but Rose was tall, plump, and solid. Her face was round and pink and she stared steady and calm from behind black-rimmed glasses. Her feet planted firmly on the wooden floor were laced into strong sensible shoes, shoes just like Susanna's. I looked from Susanna to Rose. They were alike in some way. Both sensible and practical, always knew what to do.

Rose sighed. Her voice sounded quieter than usual.

"We had such fun in here," she said. "A lot of children were evacuated. It was thought to be dangerous, so near the steelworks and the city center, but our mother wouldn't be parted from Lily. You see she'd been working hard teaching Lily to speak. It was a struggle for them both but Lily was doing well. She could make sounds that were getting close to being words. Mother was determined that the war should not interrupt all that. I was allowed to stay; Mother said that it wasn't fair to send one away and not the other."

I shuddered. "I'd hate to have been alive in the war. Weren't you afraid of the bombs?"

"Yes, we were. Especially at the beginning, but we seemed to get used to it. We felt very safe in here and all the adults made a great fuss of us as there weren't many children around. We had a special teacher come to our house and we only had lessons in the mornings."

"You lucky things," I said. Rose laughed.

"We wanted to ask you about the paintings," said Susanna.

"Yes, I thought you must be wondering why we did them. You see, at first we really quite liked the idea of having this little place at the bottom of our garden. They brought the corrugated iron bits round in lorries, and gave them out to us all. You had to dig out a few feet of soil, and set the shelter in the hole, then heap the soil back over the top. I think it worried the grown-ups, but we children thought it was good fun.

"We made it cozy with rugs and blankets, and I painted the fireplace to make it seem warm. All make-believe, but it helped. Sometimes when the siren had gone and we all had to come down here, it would be freezing. Mother would go back to the house to make hot-water bottles for us, but that was quite a dangerous thing to do.

"It was Lily who painted the garden. Even then she loved plants and flowers. She would add little bits to the picture whenever she discovered a new bud or leaf outside. You see, as I was telling your mother, Sarah, Lily and I used to sleep here in the summer for fun, not just when the siren had gone."

Susanna and I both nodded. We knew we'd have done the same.

"It almost sounds exciting, the siren and everything," I said.

"Yes, we thought so . . . it was later on that we really found out what war was all about. We'd got spoiled; perhaps we'd even got a bit careless. Every day we heard of friends or even relations being killed, but we got to feel that we were different, that it couldn't touch us. We often came down here and brought the cats."

"You had cats in here?" I said. "I've never thought what happened to cats in wartime."

"Oh yes. At first we only had one cat and we used to fight over her. Whoever had the cat was the warmest in bed. We had Poppy, such a tolerant old tabby. We used to grab her and pull her into bed. Then my mother came home with a young black kitten, Coal we called her. The idea was that we should both have a cat to keep us warm. It didn't work, though. Our old Poppy adopted young Coal and wherever Poppy went, Coal followed, so the one who got the cat was really warm; they got two cats."

"Our Stripes likes coming in here, too. Perhaps she knows about Coal and Poppy."

"I'm sure she does," said Rose. "Really the worst thing was lying awake at night thinking about food."

"Why was that?" asked Susanna. "Didn't you get enough?"

"I didn't think so," laughed Rose. "Most of the time we got enough to keep us reasonably healthy, although once I broke out in boils—that was from not getting enough vitamin C. Things were rationed: only two ounces of butter a week, two ounces of lard, two ounces of cheese. We often had only powdered egg, and sometimes the pastry was made with mineral oil."

Susanna pulled a face. "That's awful," she said. "I couldn't bear it."

"I lay awake dreaming of cream buns and chocolate éclairs. I slept here," said Rose. "Lily slept on the top."

"Yes," I said, "we knew that."

"However did you know?" asked Rose, looking hard at me—that look that told you she'd know if you lied.

It took a long time to explain, but Rose listened carefully. I gave her the note and she read it out loud.

> *"This is a secret document*
> *I am the lady of the secret place*
> *Nobody will tell*
> *My secret document will never be found.*

"I can see why you're worried about it," Rose said.

I felt a great relief. She'd taken it seriously.

"Lily wrote notes all the time and still does, but I don't remember one like this. Writing things down was very important to her. It was so hard for her when Mother died. She wouldn't try to speak anymore. None of us seemed to be able to help. She just gave up and stuck to her notes and signs. Now, I should take this note back to Lily," said Rose.

I panicked a bit.

"It'll be all right," she promised. "If it's given back to Lily, the circle will be completed, and all will be well. You know, Lily would love it if you called on her. She's ever so grateful that you helped her out when the ceiling fell down."

"Yes," I said. "We'll do that."

Rose stood up. "I'd better get back to see how that ceiling is getting on."

"Would Miss Lily like to come down here?" asked Susanna.

Rose thought for a moment. "I think it would do her good, but I don't think she could. Lily would like to visit Sarah's mother and your little Jon, who she's so fond of, but she cannot even bring herself to walk through the gate. You ask her, Susanna, but don't be disappointed if she won't."

"It's funny," I said, feeling comfortable with Rose now. "We once thought Lily was . . . well, like a witch. We were a bit frightened of her. It was so silly. I don't know how we could have thought that."

Rose gave a strange smile. "Our Lily a witch? Well, she is . . . unusual. It depends what you mean by a witch, I suppose."

Her answer shook me. I'd expected her to say, "What a silly girl," and laugh.

"We'll come and see her tomorrow, if that's all right."

"Lovely," said Rose. "I'll give her the note and explain it all. She'll be so pleased to see you."

# 9

# Miss Lily

Miss Lily saw us coming from the front room window and when we got to the door at the side she already had it open for us. I was glad about that because I'd been wondering how we'd let her know we were there, if she couldn't hear us knocking or ringing the bell.

She beckoned us into her kitchen, smiling to make us welcome, and pulled out chairs for us to sit down.

It was then that I noticed how different the kitchen looked. The only time I'd seen it was when the ceiling had fallen down and it was all a terrible mess. I hadn't really seen it then at all. Now I sat and looked, and loved what I saw. It was old-fashioned in a way, but sparkling clean. It had one of those old fireplaces that are painted black with an oven beside them. There wasn't a fire now, as the weather was too warm, but paper and coals were laid in the grate, all ready for a fire with just the striking of a match.

Miss Lily pointed to the ceiling where we could see a neat patch of new plaster. It looked quite small; you wouldn't have believed that little bit could have caused such trouble.

Close to the fireplace, still suspended quite securely, was a wooden drying rack with fresh clean clothes hung neatly across.

There was a delicious smell of baking biscuits, which no longer made me think of gingerbread houses but simply made my mouth water. There were shelves of delicate flowered crockery and on one small shelf were two red china doll-sized teacups, white inside with gold around the rims. There were two saucers and two plates to match, a small chipped jug, and a teapot. I knew at once that this was the dolls' tea set that they'd kept in our shelter. It had survived the war and was now a treasured keepsake, not for use, just for memories.

Miss Lily went to the sideboard and brought back a small white candle. She placed it on the table between Susanna and me. We sat and watched and waited, wondering what she was up to. It seemed like a ceremony of some kind, like birthday candles, but more serious. She struck a match and lit the candle, then we watched her return to the sideboard for something else. I saw with a jump that it was the old note, the one I had found. She patted my shoulder and smiled to reassure me, carefully laying the note on the table. Then from a pocket in her frock she brought out a notepad and a pencil, but frowned a little and pushed them back. She returned to the sideboard and this time brought out a fountain pen and some expensive

writing paper. She wrote in her careful loopy writing that
we now knew so well:

*I am the lady of the secret place*
*My secret document is returned to me*
*All is well.*

She stood back so that we could both read it; then
while we watched wide-eyed she held the old note up to the
candle flame and burned it, starting at one corner and only
dropping the last tiny pieces as it turned to ash.

I watched the faded sheet flare up quickly and vanish.
All my worries about finding the note vanished with it in
the flickering flame.

Susanna and I smiled with happy relief and Miss Lily
made a sign with an invisible cup and saucer and silently
made the word *tea* with her lips. Would we like a cup
of tea?

"Oh yes, please," we both said. The ceremony
was over.

Susanna went to look at a picture on the wall. She
stared for a moment, then called me over. It was an old-
fashioned painting of two little girls in white frilled dresses,
playing with Chinese lanterns. They stood among flowers
and tall grasses. Susanna pointed to the words at the bottom. It was the title of the picture. It said, "Carnation, Lily,
Lily, Rose."

"Look," said Susanna. "Their names."

Miss Lily came over and pointed to the picture. Then

she took another piece of paper from her pad and wrote, "Mother's favorite picture."

She pointed out another frame: a photograph, all in browns, of a lady with wavy hair pulled back at her neck and a lacy collar on a pleated blouse.

We knew that this was Lily and Rose's mother, and that she'd called her two daughters after her favorite picture.

"She's lovely," said Susanna. Miss Lily smiled and beckoned us back to the table, where she had put out the most delicious looking homemade biscuits and cups of tea.

Miss Lily watched our faces carefully when we spoke and so long as we looked at her she seemed to understand everything we said. She made signs to us and the shape of words with her lips, and every now and then she wrote another of her notes. We found ourselves telling her all about the shelter and how we'd made it our den.

On some of the shelves in the kitchen stood jar after jar of what looked like dried leaves. I went and had a closer look. I saw that each jar was labeled in Lily's writing. Mint. Parsley. Rosemary. Tansy. Fennel. Sage.

"Herbs," I said, "they're all herbs. I've never seen so many. My mother has a few small jars, but nothing like these."

"Let's look," said Susanna. "Some I know the name of, but not all of them. Borage. Basil. Caraway. Coriander. Oregano. I don't know these. Where did you buy them all, Miss Lily?"

She smiled and shook her head. She went over to the window and pointed outside. We both rushed to look.

We'd never seen the back garden; you couldn't see it from the front. we just stared. So many plants and flowers, all growing like mad in all directions.

"What a garden," Susanna whispered.

"Can we go out in it, please?"

Miss Lily nodded and took us out through her kitchen door, then through a wooden gate in the high bramble-covered hedge. It was like stepping into another world. I thought of Alice, when she wanted to get out into the lovely garden but couldn't, no matter how she tried. We could. We stepped through that wooden gate and right into it.

White climbing roses that were just beginning to open covered the back of the high fence. The whole garden was surrounded by a tall brick wall hung with creepers showing different shades of green. One had bright purple flowers, and another had delicate pink ones.

I breathed in wonderful smells. A small green bush gave a fresh lemony scent. There were three thick bushes of lavender, oniony-smelling chives, and sharp-scented rosemary.

Miss Lily pushed past me and pointed to a huge, bushy green plant, with tiny purple-blue flowers. At first I just thought it was a lovely bush, but then I caught a movement and saw that lying sleepy and contented right plonk in the middle was our Stripes.

"Well, you cheeky cat," I said.

She opened one lazy eye and looked at me, then she suddenly got to her feet, surprised and guilty, stretching herself and purring like mad.

"This is where she comes," said Susanna. "You said she was never at home in the day."

"You cheeky thing," I said, picking her up and stroking her head.

Miss Lily tickled her on her favorite spot, behind her ears.

"Does she come here every day?"

Miss Lily nodded and pointed to the blue flowers.

"They're really pretty," I said.

Out came the notepad and pencil. *"Catnip,"* she wrote.

I showed Susanna. "Catnip. Do cats really like it?" Lily picked a little bunch and our Stripes jumped out of my arms and pounced on it. Lily crushed the flowers and Stripes pushed her nose into them, sniffing like mad, then started to roll about, throwing the blue shoots wildly into the air.

Susanna and I both stared. "I wish we had some of that in our garden," I said.

We wandered around the lovely garden, Stripes winding round our legs. We touched leaves and flowers, admiring it all. The plants were not yet in full bloom, but I'd never seen such fresh, strong, shooting green leaves, covered with buds, almost ready to burst into flower. We knew now why Miss Lily didn't need to buy her herbs.

"I wish I knew the names," said Susanna.

"I know a few, but there's lots I don't."

Lily pulled her pad from her pocket to show that she'd write them down for us.

"Oh, Miss Lily," said Susanna. "You'd be worn out if you wrote them all for us."

Miss Lily smiled, then she flicked her forehead to tell us that she'd had an idea. She took Susanna's arm and made signs for us both to follow her back into the kitchen. She reached up to a shelf and brought down a thick loose-leaf binder, the kind my dad keeps his lists of books in. She carried it carefully to the table and pulled out chairs for us. She pointed to me.

"Shall I look?" I asked. She held up her thumb to show I'd got the right idea.

"Plants," said Susanna. "It's just what we need."

On every page was a beautiful picture of a plant and beside each one in Lily's writing was its name and its uses.

"Here's one we've seen," said Susanna. "Little flowers like daisies. 'Feverfew: cures headaches and migraine.'"

"Here's the one with big leaves and flowers like bells. 'Comfrey: a remedy for sprains and bruises.'"

Susanna was staring hard at the picture and pointed to a squiggle below. I looked carefully. "L.M.," it said. Susanna looked at me, then grinned over my shoulder at Miss Lily.

"L.M.," she said. "Lily Morgan. Lily has painted these herself."

I stared at the tiny signature, then looked around at Miss Lily. She smiled.

"But they're lovely," I said. "They're quite perfect."

Just then the doorbell rang and a red light flashed on and off.

We jumped, then laughed as we realized that this was how Lily knew when someone arrived. The light flashed until Lily opened the door. Our Jon catapulted into the room, grinning like mad and making thumbs-up signs to Lily.

When he saw us, he suddenly stopped, all surprised.

"What are you doing here?" He thumped me in the stomach then threw his arms around Susanna's waist.

"Aaah," said Susanna, "he's so lovely." She bent down and he rubbed his nose against hers. "I wish he was my brother," she said. I thought it was disgusting.

When at last we decided that it was time to go home, Miss Lily held up her hand to stop us for a moment. She fetched a small straw basket from the sideboard and gently lifted the delicate dolls' china into it. She picked a carefully written note from her kitchen drawer and held it out to me.

It said, "Thank you for bringing help when the ceiling fell in. I want you to have these little cups. They belong in your den."

"I promise I'll take great care of them," I said as we stepped down from her door.

"Miss Lily," said Susanna, then stopped, looking shy. "Miss Lily," she tried again, "please . . . would you come to see our den?"

Miss Lily suddenly looked sad, but she gave Susanna a quick hug to show that she wasn't offended. As she turned away to close the door after us, she pulled her fist up to her chest, her knuckles standing out white with strain.

# ᐃ 10 ᐅ

# A Different Kind of Magic

The Whitsuntide holidays came to an end and we had to go back to school. The weather got warmer. We kept on visiting Lily and Rose, watching their garden grow. You wouldn't have thought the plants could grow much more, but they did, and by the end of July the garden was filled with flowers and butterflies and delicious smells.

The last few weeks of the summer term seemed to whizz past. We had outings, sports, and lots of messing around. We were really looking forward to the summer holidays, because our mums had said that we could sleep in the shelter then.

So, on the Friday night that we got out, we made them stick to their promise.

"When I said the summer holidays, I didn't mean the very same night that you finished," my mum complained.

"Oh, Mum," I begged. "We've wanted to sleep in there for ages. You did say the holidays."

"Oh . . . go on," she agreed.

We carried in our sleeping bags and some rugs, dressing gowns, and slippers, and went to say good-night to our parents.

"But it's only eight o'clock," my dad said. "It's not even dark yet."

"Well, you're always trying to get me to go to bed early."

Dad laughed. "Go on. You're mad, the pair of you."

We took hot-water bottles in, just in case, but we needn't have bothered. It was lovely and cozy with the blackout curtain drawn, and Stripes followed us in.

"Just like Rose and Lily's cat," said Susanna.

I thought we'd giggle and talk till late into the night but somehow the den was so cozy and comfortable that we fell asleep quite early, and before we knew it, Mum was opening the door, bringing cups of tea. It was morning.

We decided we'd stay there every night while we were off from school. It felt like it was going to be the best holiday ever.

Sometimes we did lie awake till late, talking and talking, and we often seemed to get round to talking about Lily and Rose. It was strange, but sometimes we almost felt as though we were them. Not the grown-up Lily and Rose, but those two children who'd slept here during the war.

I was just drifting off one night when Susanna started.

"I say, Sarah, are you asleep?"

"I nearly was."

"Can you remember what you used to say about Lily? You used to say she was a witch."

"Yes," I said. "You used to say it, too."

"Suppose I did," admitted Susanna. "I know we were silly of course, but you know there are some things about her that are a bit strange, a bit witchlike. Not horrid things, like . . . well, eating children and being ugly, and . . ."

"And wearing a big black hat," I said, and giggled.

Susanna giggled, too. "Perhaps I'm dreaming it," she said.

I thought for a moment and rolled onto my back. "No . . . you're not dreaming it," I said. "I've seen her doing things, sort of magical, but a different kind of magic. I meant to tell you, but it's only a small thing, almost not worth mentioning. The other day I was round there in the garden with Lily and our Stripes, and Lily was tying some string across the sticks for the sweet peas. Well, I've never seen sweet peas like they've got. I asked Lily why they were so big and she just wrote one word on her notepad. 'Muck,' it said."

Susanna laughed. "Muck. That's not very magical."

"No," I said. "No, that's not the bit I meant to tell you about. It was what she was doing after that. She was talking to the sweet peas. Not with words of course, but her lips were moving and she was sort of making signs. Some of the flowers were leaning right out with their little curly bits just waving about. Lily was sort of telling them and showing them that they should curl their little tendrils round the string and pull themselves up on it."

"Well," said Susanna, "I've heard of people talking to

plants before. It's meant to make them grow better, I think."

"Yes, yes, I know about that," I said, "but I still haven't told you the whole thing. You see, just after that, Lily and I went in and had a cup of tea and one of her famous biscuits. It can't have taken more than ten minutes, a quarter of an hour at the most, but when we went out again they'd done it."

"Done what?"

"The sweet peas. They'd done what she'd told them to do. They'd curled their little green tendrils round the string and pulled themselves up."

"No!"

"Fifteen minutes it took them. I know it's not a big magical thing, but it quite surprised me. And another thing: have you seen Lily catch the butterflies?"

"Yes," said Susanna. "I've tried to do it, but I can't. She just puts out her hand and catches them in full flight, then she sort of gives them a little whisper and opens her hand and off they fly, fluttering round her head. She does it so slowly, no rushing, so gentle, as though it were the most natural thing to do. And of course there's your Stripes; she just does everything Miss Lily wants."

"Yes," I said. "She won't do what I want. Will you, naughty cat?" I tickled the furry chin stretched up to me, for Stripes had crept purring onto my stomach as though she knew we were talking about her.

"There's something else," I said. "When Lily burned that old note I found, I felt as though something a bit magical happened then. As the note was burned, I suddenly felt happy and free. I knew I needn't worry anymore about having found it."

"Yeah," Susanna agreed. "It was a strange thing to do, anyway. Most people would have just thrown it in the trash. She made it seem special, a different kind of magic."

"Could she really be a witch?" I wondered.

"I thought there was no such thing as witches," said Susanna. "I used to be frightened when I was little and I heard those stories, but my mother told me, 'There's no such thing as witches.' "

"Yeah, I've heard people say that, too, but once I saw something in one of my dad's books, something about witches being burned. It all sounded horrid, but you can't burn them if there's no such thing, can you?"

Susanna was silent.

"I might look for that book again. I might ask Dad. I'll see . . ." and we drifted off to sleep.


But I did remember that conversation and I did look for that book again, but I couldn't find it.

"Dad," I said, "there was a big red book here, with curly black patterns on it."

"Yes," he said. "*History of the British Isles.* Sold it yesterday morning. What's all this sudden interest? You haven't decided to learn something, have you?"

"I learn a lot," I said. "All the time in fact. What do you think I do at school?"

"Look out the window and poke things at Susanna."

"Well, that as well," I admitted. "But about that book

. . . I just wanted to know. Was it a proper history book, about what really happened?"

"Well, as good as you'd get. Who can know what really happened?" I wish my dad wouldn't say things like that. It makes you feel confused, just when you think you're getting things sorted out.

"Why?" he asked. "You're not turning into a bookworm when I'd nearly given up hope?"

"Don't be silly, Dad. It was . . . the witch. I saw a picture, a horrid picture—a witch getting burned."

"And it frightened you?" Dad suddenly stopped teasing and got serious.

"No. Well, it did look frightening, but what I wanted to know was, are there such things as witches?"

He frowned and thought for a moment.

"I think it depends on what you mean by a witch. If you mean the kind in stories, old and ugly, dressed in black . . . no, there were no such people. They were put into stories to frighten children. Make 'em do what they're told. Mind you," he said, grinning again, "I could do with something to make 'em do as they're told."

I thought that was all the serious information I'd get out of my dad, but just as I was going out of the shop he called out to me.

"Of course Rose is the one you should ask. Rose is the expert on witches."

I turned and looked back at him. My mouth must have dropped open, because he laughed at my expression. A shiver ran down my back, then I went straight back to find Susanna and tell her what he'd said.

## 11

# Which Kind of Witch?

It was Sunday when we next went round to see Rose and Lily. We went specially on Sunday, as we knew Rose would be there.

We found it very interesting seeing Rose and Lily together. We watched with amazement as Lily talked to Rose. I say talked; she actually made signs and the expression on her face helped to show what she meant. You wouldn't believe how fast she did it.

Gradually we began to learn a few signs. Thumbs up, to say hello. Holding your hands in front and pulling them toward yourself meant welcome, come in. We realized that a lot of the waving about our Jon did was actually proper signing that he'd picked up from Lily. But Lily signing to Rose was really something. We stared openmouthed, she did it so fast, and we couldn't catch it at all, but Rose did; she understood every bit.

There didn't seem to be any other way to ask Rose

about witches, so we just asked her straight.

"Rose," I said, "my dad says you're an expert on witches."

"Does he indeed," said Rose, laughing. "No one's ever called me that before."

"Are you though?" asked Susanna. "It's just that we really wanted to know."

"It must be all those books," said Rose. "I suppose I've bought all the books your dad's ever had on the subject."

"But isn't it frightening?" I asked.

Rose thought for a moment. "No," she said. "It's interesting and it's sad but not frightening, not that."

I wanted to ask so many questions but didn't know which to start with and it all seemed to tumble out at once. Susanna asked lots, too.

"But are there real witches?"

"Why were they burned?"

"What did they do?"

"Were they wicked?"

Rose just laughed. "You really *do* want to know. That's wonderful; I love talking about it, my pet subject. Come upstairs to my secret library. I'll show you some of my books."

Rose mouthed over our heads to Lily, and we followed her upstairs. We hadn't been upstairs in their house before and that was interesting, too, because their house was exactly the same as ours with even the staircase on the same side. The bathroom was at the top of the stairs, two big bedrooms back and front, and then a little bedroom at the front. Just the same, but really different.

On their stair wall they had big framed pictures of ladies wearing long white dresses, where we've got bright modern posters with triangles and dots, that my mum collects. They had lovely flowery wallpaper around their landing, where ours is painted plain white on gritty-looking wallpaper.

The two big rooms were their bedrooms. Rose took us into the small room at the front. It really was a secret library. The walls were covered with bookshelves. There was nothing else in the room, just bookshelves full of books. It smelled just like my dad's shop and I kept noticing book covers that looked familiar.

"Oh, I've never seen so many," said Susanna. "Not in someone's own house."

"Where did you get all the shelves?" I asked.

"Made 'em," said Rose. "Lily helped. Now, ask away. What was it you wanted to know?"

"We know there's no such thing as witches like the ones in fairy stories. Horrid, ugly old things who ate children and rode on broomsticks, but my dad seemed to think there might be some other kind."

"I expect he means the wise women. Yes, they were very real. Every village had one."

"But what did they do?"

"Tried their best to cure all ills. They grew herbs and made medicines that often worked well. After all, there were no proper doctors then and even when there were, ordinary people couldn't afford to pay them. The wise women were all they had."

"So they weren't wicked then?" Susanna looked relieved.

"Just as good or bad as anyone else, I should think. They gave all kinds of advice and help. People consulted them about their children, their animals, the weather. I think they probably did have special knowledge that they passed down to their daughters, so it stayed in the family."

"But why did people burn them?" I asked. It sounded to me as if they were only trying to be helpful and useful.

Rose looked serious and I could see it really mattered to her.

"That's what I mean by the sad bit. People were afraid of them, and if the cures didn't work, the wise women got the blame. And of course the cures couldn't always work."

"So they killed them if something went wrong?" That seemed terrible to me.

"I think that did happen sometimes," said Rose, "but sometimes it was even worse than that. Most of the women who were killed weren't even the wise women or witches. They were just ordinary women who people wanted to get rid of. There have been certain times in the past when there were witch-hunts. People got really silly and wild, and anyone who was just called a witch could be killed: old women who were a nuisance; young women who'd caused jealousy; anyone who was unusual or odd in some way."

I thought of Lily and how I'd called her a witch because she was deaf and I didn't understand her. I felt horrid.

"In Scotland they burned them, but in England they were hung," continued Rose. "In Pendle, in Lancastershire, there was a famous case. Nineteen so-called witches were hung, and mainly on the evidence of a poor half-witted young girl."

"Stop," I said. "I can't bear it. I called Lily a witch," I said.

"It was me, too," said Susanna, and she linked her arm through mine. We both stared at Rose, guilty and miserable.

She stared back, but she smiled.

"Lily would be happy to be called a witch," Rose said. "She'd be glad to think she was like those wise women in the past. She grows herbs, and studies their uses. She has a special way with plants—green fingers you might say. There are lots of things Lily just knows. She follows her instincts and she's nearly always right. I try to copy her."

"So are you a witch?" Susanna asked.

Rose laughed. "I try to be, I try."

"So being a witch is all right," I said.

"I think we've all got a bit of witchiness in us," said Rose. "At least, we have if we let ourselves, if we look for it, if we follow our instincts."

"You mean . . . even us?" I said.

"Even you." Rose nodded. Susanna and I grinned.


We looked at some of Rose's books. We saw a list of well-known local witches in olden times. Bessy Slack of West Burton, Nanny Pearson of Goathland, the Guisborough witch Anne Grear, Old Sally Scree of Skeltondale. The best known of all was Mother Shipton of Knaresborough, said Rose.

We looked at books full of beautiful pictures of herbs and plants—we could see where Lily had got her ideas from.

"People who lived thousands of years ago were much closer to the earth than we are," said Rose. "I think we have something to learn from them. We should respect and care for our earth, not fill it with rubbish and pollution."

"But did they have magic?" Susanna asked.

"Only the magic that's all around us. The magic that brings the sun and fresh green shoots each spring. I think they saw each season as magical. We seem to take it all for granted now."

I thought of their lovely garden and nodded my head, beginning to understand what she meant.


Later that night in the shelter we talked about it again.

"If Miss Lily is like a witch, or has a bit of witchiness as Rose calls it, why is she still so sad about her mother? So sad that she can't come down here?"

"You'd think she could cure herself, wouldn't you?" Susanna said.

"Perhaps it's harder to cure yourself," I said. "But I know what you mean. She's really so clever, isn't she? You know that class she goes to? Well, Rose told me that it's a class for deaf people and their teachers, to help them learn to sign. Lily doesn't go to learn; she's the teacher. Rose said that Lily's really the best person in our city for teaching sign language. So you'd think someone so . . . so capable would have got over her mother's death all that time ago."

"Yes," said Susanna. "But I've noticed that whenever it's mentioned, she closes up her fist so tight and pulls it to her chest, and Rose told me that is the sign for feeling guilty. I think that's the trouble. She just can't stop feeling guilty about what happened, and I wish she could."

I looked down at Susanna in her bunk. She does notice things about people, I thought.

"I wish she could, too," I said.

# 12

# A Day in the Country

The first few weeks of the holidays whizzed by. The weather was hot and Susanna and I spent a lot of time at the Lido in our park.

Rose and Lily's garden bloomed and blossomed. We helped them pick the herbs and saw how they tied up bundles, wrapped around with paper, then hung them up to dry. Lily picked flowers to make into potpourri. I'd seen it in little jars in the shops but I'd never seen any like Lily made. Every flower you could imagine went into it, and she made different kinds. My favorite was a mixture of lavender, catnip, rosemary, and lovely bright blue cornflowers that kept their strong color even when dried. She gave us a big bowlful to keep in our den. It smelled great, and when we walked past we stirred it with our fingers and it let out a new fresh burst of scent each time.

66

You wouldn't think you could actually get fed up with enjoying yourself, but eventually we did.

The middle of August was very hot and dry. We couldn't go away anywhere as Dad insisted on keeping his shop open every day and said we couldn't afford to, anyway.

Susanna's parents couldn't afford to, either. They said they'd spent all their money on moving house. I was secretly glad of that; at least I had Susanna to be with. Jennifer Wainwright had gone off to Majorca for three weeks, and she'd been showing off all her new holiday clothes for three weeks before that.

Susanna and I went down to the Lido as usual, and, coming back, we walked past the bumper cars and the little kids throwing themselves about on the bouncy castle.

"Shall we go on the bumper cars again?" Susanna asked.

I pulled a face. "I haven't enough money left, anyway."

I looked out at the playground with the swings and slides and that push-along roundabout that makes you dizzy.

"If I go on that roundabout one more time, I'll scream," I said.

Susanna nodded. "It's got boring, hasn't it?"

"Yes," I said, and sat down on the park bench. "I'm bored, bored, bored."

"Two more weeks and we'll be back in school," said Susanna. "That'll be worse."

"S'pose it will."

We sat there for ages just kicking our feet in the dust and squeezing trickles of wet from our hair. Gary Fox and his gang started jumping off the climbing frame behind us so we decided to go.

As we walked home past the library, we thought we'd stop in to see Rose. It seemed better than going straight back. Rose took one look at us and smiled.

"Holidays wearing you out?"

"We're bored," I said. "We don't know what to do."

"I'll find you a job. Plenty of books to mend, and I need the science section moved over to that corner."

We pulled a face at each other.

Rose laughed. "Sometimes it's good to be bored," she said. "Then, when something interesting or exciting happens, you really enjoy it and notice the difference."

"Nothing exciting ever happens," I said.

"Well, not just now," Susanna added.

"Something will happen," said Rose, "and it will happen when you least expect it."

We both smiled at that. It sounded like one of Rose's witchy predictions.

"Well, I hope you're right," I said.


I knocked on Susanna's door early the next morning.

"I've got to go to a book fair," I said. "Dad's got a stall at it, somewhere out in the country. Do you want to come?"

"I'll have to tell Mum."

I followed her into the house.

"It'll be boring," I said, "but I suppose it's something to do."

"Skeltondale," said Susanna's mother. "Oh, that's a lovely village. You'll enjoy yourselves. That'll be a real day out."

"Well, last time we went to a book fair it was awful," I said. "Mum and Dad were so busy with the stall, they just kept giving our Jon money for fizzy drinks and ice cream, and on the way back he was sick all over me."

"Ugh," said Susanna. "He'd better not do that today."

"He was sick over Dad's box of valuable ancient books, too," I said. "So you can imagine what Dad was like."

It was quite a long ride to Skeltondale and it was a bit crowded in the back of our van, with our Jon and Susanna and huge boxes of books sticking into my back.

"I keep thinking I've been to Skeltondale before," said Susanna, "or perhaps I've just heard of it."

"Yes," I said, "I thought I'd heard something about it but I can't think what."

"It's really pretty," said Mum. "It's very old and built round a wide green with a stream running through it, and sheep wander all around, nibbling at the grass."

"I'll chase them sheep," said Jon.

"No you won't," said Mum. "There's a museum that's quite well known. The girls can take you to look round it."

We both groaned.

Dragging Jon around a stuffy old museum sounded terrible.

Actually, Skeltondale did turn out to be good. It was a big village, and very pretty—the sort of place that's full of summer visitors. It was sunny and we left Mum and Dad setting up the stall and took Jon down to the stream to paddle. Mum had been right about the sheep; they were everywhere. We laughed like mad because whenever a sheep came near our Jon, he ran and hid behind me or Susanna.

We had a picnic with crisps and lemonade and Cornish pasties, then homemade ice cream from one of the village shops.

"Take our Jon to look at the museum," said Mum.

"Oh, do we have to? They're going to do morris dancing outside the pub. We want to watch that."

"I want to go to museum," Jon whined.

"Oh, well, I suppose I could take you," said Mum. "Dad can cope by himself for a while."

Susanna and I walked down to the pub. We weren't specially interested in the morris dancing but it was quite funny to watch big men in flowery hats, with bells on their legs, jumping up and down and waving their handkerchiefs in the air.

Jon came back later on and sat down beside us. He looked a bit serious, a bit worried.

"What's wrong?" said Susanna. "Didn't you like the museum?"

Jon just shook his head and said, "Poor witch."

"What?" I said. "What did you say?"

Jon turned a solemn face to me. "Poor witch," he said. "In that museum, there's a poor witch."

Susanna suddenly looked across at me. "That's it," she said. "A witch. That's where we've heard about Skeltondale. It was in Rose's book, the one about real witches. It said there was a real witch who lived at Skeltondale."

I knew she was right and a great burst of excitement shot through me. I remembered Rose's words. "Something will happen, and it will happen when you least expect it."

"We'd better go and look at this museum after all," I said.

"I'm coming, too," said Jon. "I want to see poor witch again."

# ⚓ 13 ⚓

# The Witch Is in Her Den

The museum was much better than we'd expected, right from the start. We walked into a room full of people. Some were visitors like us, walking around. Others were life-sized models sitting at a huge table, ready to eat a harvest supper. They all wore olden-days clothes, sort of country olden-days clothes. The food they were to eat looked real and mouthwatering, although when you looked closely you could see it was made out of clay and wax. Next to the harvest supper were more model people dancing in a ring, dancing around a sheaf of corn.

"Witch isn't in here," said Jon, tugging at my skirt.

We walked on and found a room full of old children's toys. Sets of tiny cups and plates, even toy food, were set at tables in dolls' houses; a whole miniature world.

Jon still pulled me along. "Stop it," I said, "don't rush me. It's interesting."

"Here it is," said Susanna, peeping into the next room. "Here's lots about witches."

"No," yelled Jon. "Witch isn't here."

But Susanna was right. We saw a witch's magic book that she had used for weather predictions, and a board with pictures and squares that had been used for giving advice and telling the future. There was even a crystal ball that a witch had looked into. Next to this was a long list of witches known in the area: Nanny Pearson of Goathland; Auld Mother Migg of Cropton, who did use a crystal ball; Sally Scree of Skeltondale. . . .

"That's her," I said, pointing to the name. "That's the one in Rose's book."

"I think they were all in Rose's book," Susanna said. "Rose would like this museum, wouldn't she?"

"Yes, but what would she think of that? It says there's one who changed herself into a cat, and another who changed herself into a hare."

"She'd just laugh at that."

"Look," I said, "she'd agree with this. 'Dolly Millbank of Danby, greatly skilled in the curing of ailments, and wrought she many wonderful cures.' "

"Yes," said Susanna. "That's just the sort of witch she admires."

"Where's our Jon?" I said.

Susanna looked around. "He was here a minute ago."

"Oh no, he's always doing this. He just runs off where he wants and I have to go traipsing around looking for him."

"He'll have gone to find this 'poor witch' he kept on about. Hadn't we better look for him?"

"Yes," I said. "S'pose we should."

I knew Mum and Dad would be furious if we went

back without him. We went round calling his name, but it was embarrassing and we still couldn't find him.

The rest of the museum things were really interesting. There were cottages that you could walk into, full of old-fashioned furniture, and there was a lovely, bright, painted gypsy caravan. I wanted to stop and look but I couldn't, what with our Jon being so naughty. Then Susanna saw him at last. He was standing in front of a small thatched hut. There was a window at the side and a closed doorway with a peephole in it. Jon was jumping up and down, trying to see inside. He turned around and saw us coming toward him.

"Lift me up, lift me up," he demanded.

"I don't see why we should." I gave him a shove. "Running off like that and making us go all over looking for you."

"At least we've found him," said Susanna, and she picked him up.

He took no notice of me, just poked his head through the peephole in the door.

"Aah," he said. "Poor witch."

"Let me see," I said, feeling impatient.

You could really only look in one at a time because your head filled up the hole, but Susanna pushed her face up close to Jon and managed to peep in with him.

They both stared silently through the hole and I got really fed up. I gave them both a push, then stuck my head through instead.

It was really quite a shock; two gray eyes stared back at me. The hut was very dark inside and at first I saw only the witch's face standing out in the dim light. But then, as my eyes got used to it, I saw her tall black hat and long black dress. She was leaning on a broomstick and stood beside a huge black caldron. At her feet a fierce black cat arched its back.

I shuddered. It was the witch of Hansel and Gretel, the witch of Rapunzel—evil, ugly, and so sad. Her eyes were light gray with deep black centers. They seemed very real, and they made me catch my breath. Her face and hands were clearly papier-mâché that had been painted and varnished, but her eyes. . . . It was as though a real person looked out from them.

"Let me see poor witch again." Jon pulled at my arm.

I stood back and picked him up. I didn't feel cross with him anymore. I looked over at Susanna.

"You can see why he says 'poor witch,' " she said.

We took turns at lifting Jon until our arms ached, then he ran around to the side to look into the lower window; he could see the witch's side view from there. We peeped in the door again. I stared into those eyes and suddenly gasped, realizing that they reminded me of Miss Lily's eyes: gray, farseeing, and very sad—like Lily looked when she thought about her mother.

I turned to Susanna. "She makes me think of . . ."

"Yes," said Susanna. "Miss Lily. I know."

Susanna looked again.

"She hasn't got much in her hut, has she? The walls are bare and the floor is all dirty."

"Yes," I said. "A real witch would have lots of things in her den. She'd have loads of jars to make her medicines."

"Yes. She'd have to have shelves and cupboards to keep her bottles and mixtures on."

"She'd have to have a sink," said Susanna, "and all the ordinary things you need for living, and I don't see why it should be so dirty. She'd have to keep it all clean."

"Yes," I said. "If she didn't keep it clean, she'd poison everyone, and she wouldn't last long then."

Susanna suddenly looked really pleased and excited. "Wouldn't it be good," she said, "to make a real witch's den, with bottles and herbs, and a crystal ball and magic books."

"Oooh yes. It'd be great, but where . . . ?" and I stopped and smiled, because I'd realized where. "In our den, of course. We can turn our den into a real witch's den."

Susanna grinned and nodded.

"We could make a real witch," said Susanna. "Not with all those black clothes. We'd have to think what a proper witch would wear."

"It'd be hard to make a figure," I said. "It'd take a lot of papier-mâché."

We both thought for a moment and Susanna looked in at the museum witch again, then she turned back to me.

"No," she said. "We don't need to make a witch. What did Rose say? We all have a bit of witchiness, if we want it. We are the witches. We don't need a papier-mâché one."

I nodded. "Yes. We are the witches, you and me. I can't wait to get home and get started."

We suddenly realized the time. Mum and Dad would be packing up the stall and wondering where we were. We persuaded Jon to leave "poor witch" by telling him, "We're going to make our air-raid shelter into a witch's den, and you can come and see it."

We talked about it all the way home in the back of our van, and Mum and Dad kept grinning at each other. "I think they've really enjoyed their day out," Mum said.

# ⤜ 14 ⤏

# A Bit of Healing,
# a Bit of Magic

We started work early the next morning. First we gave our den a really good clean-out. Then we searched in our houses for all the old bottles and jam jars that we could find. We went round to see Miss Lily and told her all about it. She understood just what we wanted to do. She took us into her garden and helped us to pick big bunches of her herbs. We took sage, rosemary, thyme, lavender, and a lovely strong-smelling herb called curry plant.

We hammered nails into the top beams and hung the herbs in bundles from the ceiling. Wonderful smells filled the den. We worked all morning to get those things done.

After lunch, we cut up cardboard boxes, and painted different colored squares on them, with pictures like the ones on the witch's board that we'd seen. Things to do with nature really: the moon, sun, stars, flowers, wavy lines for water, and, of course, a cat.

We wanted a crystal ball but we couldn't think what we could use; then we found our old goldfish bowl in the cellar. My dad kept nails in it. We tipped out the nails, washed it, and turned it upside down, and it looked just right, quite magical. When you put it under the light, wavy patterns appeared, and when you lifted it up, you could see the whole den and us upside down and sort of rounded. It was fascinating. I could see why staring into a crystal ball could be helpful; it could make you see the whole world as a better, magical place.

"What about us?" I asked Susanna. "We've got to think what witches would wear. Not black hats, we know that, but what would we wear instead?"

"Well," said Susanna, "if witches were busy people, always making things and gardening, I think they'd have to wear sensible clothes. Those black hats would keep falling off, wouldn't they? They wouldn't worry about fashion but I think they'd wear aprons to keep them-selves clean, and have big pockets to keep their bits and pieces in."

I thought that sounded okay, and we found aprons with pockets in. Mine was a flowery one that my mum never wore. Susanna's was a plain one of her own. I felt a bit disappointed and thought we just looked like two daft girls with aprons over their jeans.

"We don't look special enough," I said. "We need something to make us look good. Witches like plants and herbs and flowers. That's what we need."

Susanna agreed, so we raided our garden and Miss Lily's again. We made ourselves garlands of flowers and fresh herbs, fastening them into our hair. That seemed much better. We sat down at the table, with our magic boards and crystal ball, to admire our witch's den.

"What I really wish now is that we could go and get Miss Lily to come and see it," I said. "She's helped us so much . . . I wish she could come here. When we took the herbs this morning she followed us right to our gate. For a moment I thought she was going to come."

Susanna looked at me all thoughtful but she never spoke. Then she got up and fetched a bit of paper and a pen.

"What's wrong?" I said. "What are you going to do?"

"The time is right," she said, all serious.

She started to write. I could see she was doing it carefully, her best writing, not rushed or sloppy. I got up and went around behind her to see what she'd written.

*The time is right*
*The lady of the secret place will return*
*All will be well.*

"Why have you written that?" I said. "What are you going to do?"

She wouldn't answer. She stood up.

"You're not going to give that to Miss Lily," I said.

Slowly she nodded. "It's the notes," she said. "The notes made me think. Writing things down . . . that's important to Miss Lily."

"But you can't do that," I said. "It might upset her."

Susanna went to the door, but hesitated. I could see she nearly changed her mind. "Follow your instincts, that's what Rose said. I just know that the time is right."

Then, as though she was afraid she'd change her mind if she just walked, she ran up the steps and down the side of our house. I followed behind her. I couldn't believe what she was doing; she was usually so sensible and quiet.

I just got to Miss Lily's gate as Susanna came flying back, red-faced and out of breath. She ran past me and back to our house, back to our witch's den. She was sitting at the table when I got there. She looked terrible, flushed and worried. All on edge.

"Leave the curtain open," she said, quite sharp.

"Where did you put it?" I asked.

"Through her letter-box," she said. "Then I rang the doorbell . . . and ran away."

We both just sat there at our table. It seemed like ages, but then we heard a slight noise on the steps. We both stared at the doorway, and our Stripes walked in with a greeting meow. We both grinned, but then a shadow blocked the light. Miss Lily stood at the entrance.

I held my breath. I daren't move or make a sound but Susanna stood up; she knew exactly what she was doing. She made the sign, pulling her hands toward her chest, the sign that meant welcome.

Miss Lily ducked her head and stepped inside. I knew then it was going to be all right.

Lily sat down on the bottom bunk. She looked around tense at first, but at last her face relaxed. She took up the pen Susanna had left on our table and she wrote:

> The lady of the secret place has returned
> All is well.

Then she took us by the hand and smiled and smiled.

We heard a clomping in the garden, and Jon came in.

"I seen you come in here," he said, and climbed straight onto Miss Lily's lap. Then our Stripes leaped up, too. Miss Lily just smiled and made room for them both, and we all sat there happy and quiet for a while.

At last Miss Lily got up and looked at all the things we'd put in our den. She touched the flowers in our hair and signed to show that she approved. She stood for a while by the curtains, holding them in her hand.

We heard more footsteps from outside and Rose appeared, looking anxious. "Lily," she mouthed. "Are you all right?"

She saw from Lily's face that she was very much all right and the two sisters hugged each other tightly. My eyes went all watery. I smiled across at Susanna and saw that she was just the same.

The next thing was that Mum came tapping down the steps with a tray and cups of tea.

We all crammed around the little table and Rose told us that this was how it had been in our shelter during the war. People all squashed together, drinking cups of tea.

My mum had seen Lily go into the shelter and she'd rung Rose at the library. She'd felt a bit worried about her, she said.

We all told Rose what had happened and Miss Lily did a lot of signing. Rose looked very pleased.

"Well, you two witches have really done a bit of healing, a bit of magic," she said.

I kept looking across at Susanna. I still couldn't believe what she'd done. I realized that I was still only just getting to know her . . . my friend, the clever witch.

"It was Susanna that did it all," I said.

"I think it was both of you," said Rose. "You found the note and it brought us all together. I think that was a bit of magic in itself."

I bent over and tickled our Stripes in her special place behind her ears. "It was Stripes who found the note really," I said.

"Ah," said Rose. "A good witch needs a cat to help her."